Published by Modern Publishing,
a Division of Unisystems, Inc.

Designed for Modern Publishing by Victoria House
Publishing Limited, 4/5 Lower Borough Walls,
Bath, England BA1 1QR

Printed in Belgium.

Flora Goes to Town

Written by Barbara Hayes and Illustrated by Phillip Mendoza

MODERN PUBLISHING
A Division of Unisystems, Inc.
New York, New York 10022

"We have nothing to do today!"

"Well, what shall we do, Jeremy?" asked Annabel.

"We could go see the new show," suggested Jeremy.

"I'm very tired of shows," sighed Annabel.

"Well," said Jeremy, "we could drive out to the country to visit Cousins Flora and Fred."

"I know!" exclaimed Annabel. "Let's invite Flora and Fred to come here instead. They have never been to town."

Jeremy looked doubtful. "Do you think they'd enjoy themselves?" he asked.

"Don't be silly," said Annabel. "People in the country always want to visit town. I'll write them a letter right now!"

Annabel's letter arrived at Flora's the next day. Flora rushed out to find Fred.

"Fred! Fred!" she called, hurrying into the hayfield. "Cousin Annabel has invited us to stay with her in town!"

Fred looked up from his work. "Do we have to go?" he said gloomily. "I've never been to town. I don't even know what they do there."

"Don't be silly," laughed Flora. "We'll have a wonderful time with Annabel and Jeremy."

The next morning Flora and Fred woke up early.
They wanted to make sure they were on the first
train into town.

When they arrived at the train station, Flora
suggested they take a taxi. But Fred wanted to walk.

Fred and Flora knocked hard on Annabel's front
door, but no one answered.

"I hope Annabel isn't sick," said Flora, anxiously.

"Perhaps we got the dates confused," said Fred.

Finally Annabel opened the door. "You're so
early!" she gasped.

Annabel had planned lots of wonderful outings for her cousins. First she took Flora to an auction.

"Look at all the treasures," she told Flora. "Wouldn't you like one of those beautiful paintings?"

"But why would I want a painting of someone I don't know?" askcd Flora in surprise.

"Oh, well," sighed Annabel. Then Annabel decided to take Flora to her favorite hat shop.

The saleslady brought out a big pile of hats. Flora started to try them on, but she didn't seem to like any of them. Suddenly Flora saw just what she wanted.

"Why, look at this!" she cried, picking up a little hat from underneath the pile. "It reminds me of my *old* hat. What luck!"

"Oh, Flora!" cried Annabel. "It *is* your old hat!"

The next day, Annabel had a surprise for Flora. "Tonight, we will have a big party!" she declared. "Of course, you and Fred need new party clothes."

Flora was thrilled when Annabel picked out a beautiful party dress for her. But Fred wasn't interested. He was eating sandwiches in the dress shop! "I always have a snack about now on the farm," he said. Annabel just sighed.

There were many things to do before the party!
Annabel told her friends about Flora's new dress.

Imagine everyone's surprise, when Flora entered
the party wearing an apron over her lovely evening
gown!

"I didn't want to spill anything on it," Flora
whispered to Annabel.

Annabel was speechless.

Annabel was so tired of thinking of things for Flora and Fred to do, that she stayed in bed late the next morning.

She was reading the paper, when she heard snipping sounds coming from her garden. She hurried outside and saw that Fred had clipped a hedge to look just like her. "Oh, my!" she exclaimed. "I'll be the only one in town with my own hedge sculpture! Thank you, Fred!"

Fred smiled happily. "I'm best at outdoor things," he said.

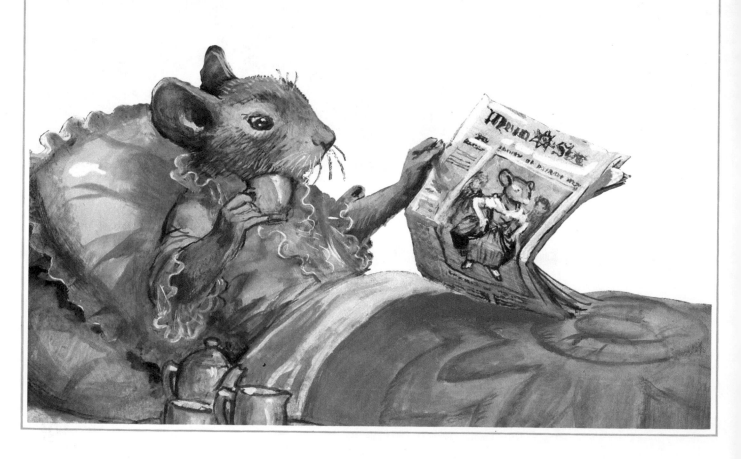

Later that afternoon, Annabel spoke to Flora and Fred. "As a special treat," she announced, "Jeremy and I are taking you both to the opera!"

"How lovely!" exclaimed Flora and Fred, wondering what an *opera* could be.

As they marched up the steps to the opera house, they heard a fiddler playing in the street.

"My uncle used to play the fiddle like that," Fred whispered to Flora. "Only we didn't have to dress up to listen to *him*."

Once they were inside Flora and Fred enjoyed the show. Fred liked the action scenes and Flora loved all the singing and the costumes.

At last it was time for Flora and Fred to go back to the country. When they got back to their peaceful little cottage, Flora baked some cakes to send to Annabel.

"Poor Annabel needs cheering up," she told Fred. "She probably wished she lived in the country."

Annabel was very pleased when the postman delivered the package. "How nice of Flora," she thought. "Flora and Fred definitely enjoyed themselves," she told Jeremy. "After all, they probably wished they lived in town."